FIX THAT CLOCK

KURT CYRUS

Houghton Mifflin Harcourt

Boston   New York

Tock . . .

      tick . . .

            Clunk!

The clock's a pile of junk.
Rusty, dusty, moldy, musty.

Tock . . .

      tick . . .

            Clunk!

Rats are nesting on the beams.
Bats are resting in the seams.
Time is rusted in the gears,
frozen fast for years and years.

Once it was a splendid sight.
All the corners angled right.
Every line was straight and true.
Now it needs a nail or two.

Tramp!

Tramp!

Tramp!

Marching up the ramp.
Up we walk to fix the clock.

Tramp!

Tramp!

Tramp!

Seven steps upon a stair.
Six are tangled, one is bare.
Five are red. Two are green.
Four are thick and three are lean.
Three are solid. Four have rot.
Two are level, five are not.
One is nailed. Six have screws.
Nothing here that we can use.
Give a jiggle. Watch them fall.
Seven steps.
Replace them all!

Creak—
Crack—
CRASH!

Ripping out the trash.
Mice are hiding in the siding . . .

Creak—
Crack—
CRASH!

Twenty mice.
It's a rout!
Ten run up.
Nine run out.
One is left.
He can't decide—

up a leg
he runs
to hide.

Bam!
Bam!
Bam!

Nails are made to slam.
Swing that hammer, Super Slammer.

Bam!
Bam!
Bam!

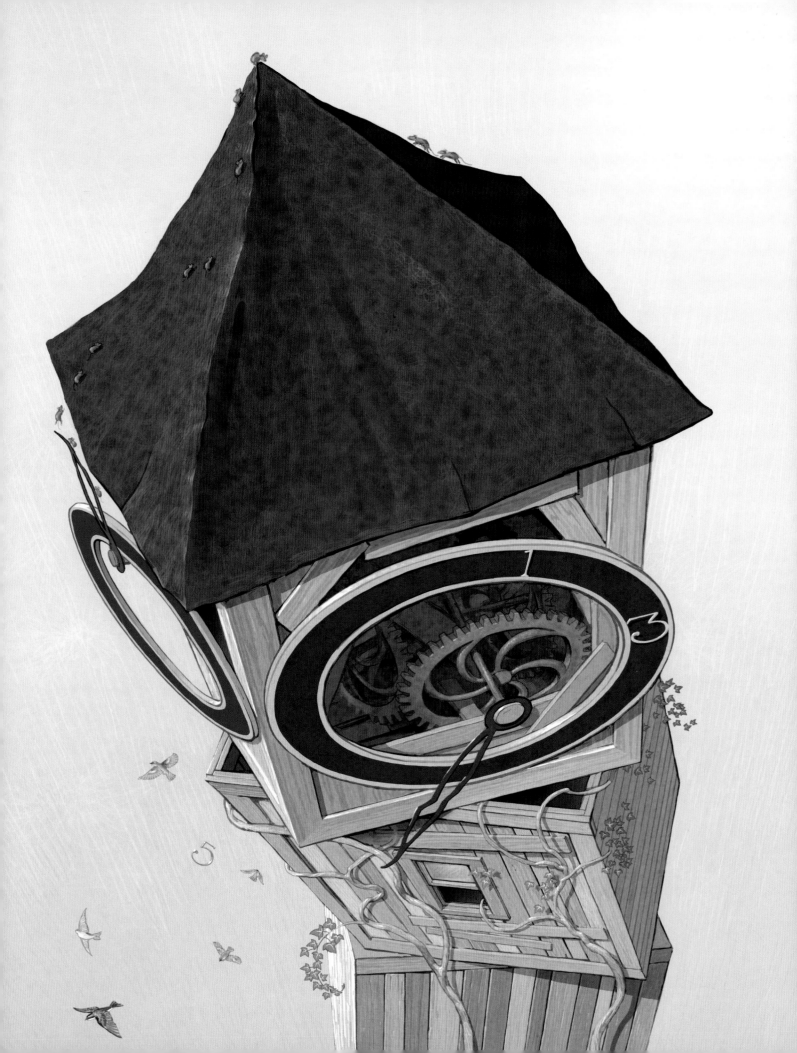

Wibble-wobble goes the clock,
shaking loose a noisy flock.
First, the flapping pigeons go;
second is the cawing crow;
third, the owl; then the bats,
swallows, sparrows, mice, and rats.
Flap and flutter! Scratch and hop!
Scramble to the tippy-top.

Four-by-fours are cut to length.
Brace them up for extra strength.
Check the angles! Make repairs!
Turn the zigzags into squares.

Put some windows here and there.
Cut a circle. Cut a square.
Wide or narrow, short or tall—
make them any shape at all.

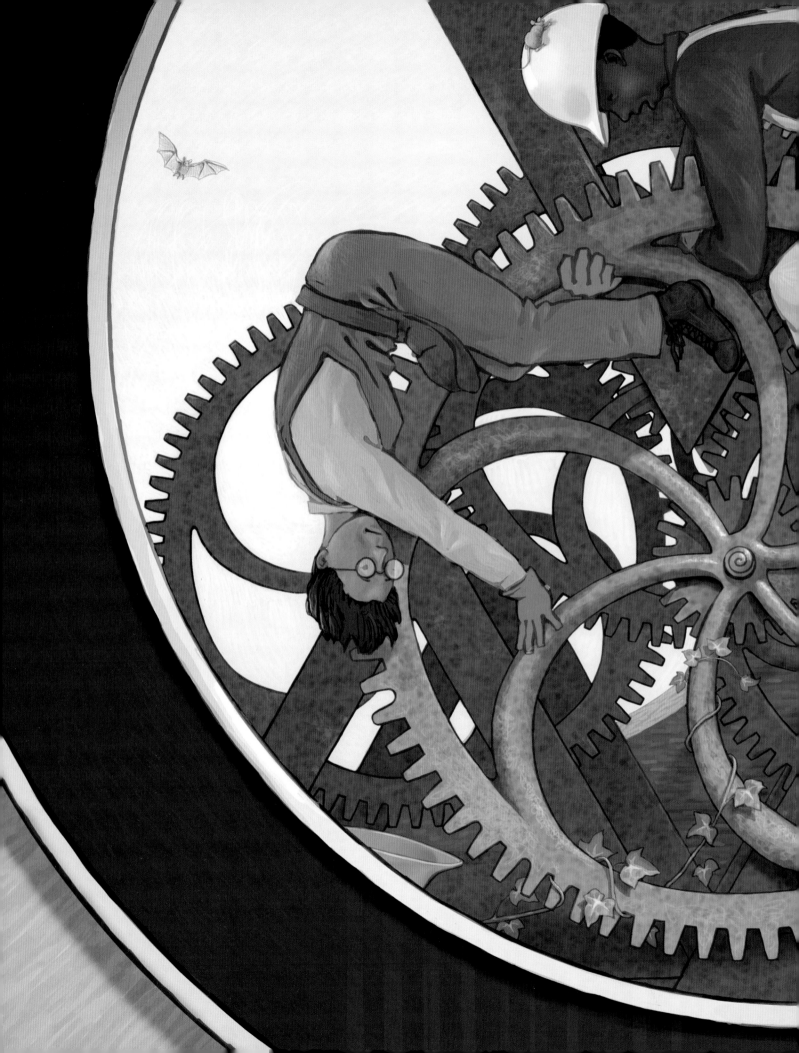

Tock . . .

tick . . .

Clank!

Give the gears a yank.
Squeaking, grinding,
creaking, binding.

Tock . . .

tick . . .

Clank!

Prime the wood.
Paint it, too.
   Pink and purple!
      Black and blue!
Sweep the dust.
Clean the glass.
Put some polish on the brass.
Hang the numbers.
Grease the gears.
Start the clock, and plug your ears—

Bong!

Bong!

The clock is chiming.
Rats and mice continue climbing.

Bong!

Bong!

The clapper rings.
Bats and pigeons lift their wings.
One more **bong** and then—
that's it.

Five o'clock.

Time to quit.

Here's a pile of extra wood.
Scraps are useful. Ends are good.
Extra nails. Extra screws . . .
these are things that we can use.

Tap.

Tap.

Tap.

Saving every scrap.
Nailing, screwing, drilling, gluing.

Tap.

Tap.

Tap.

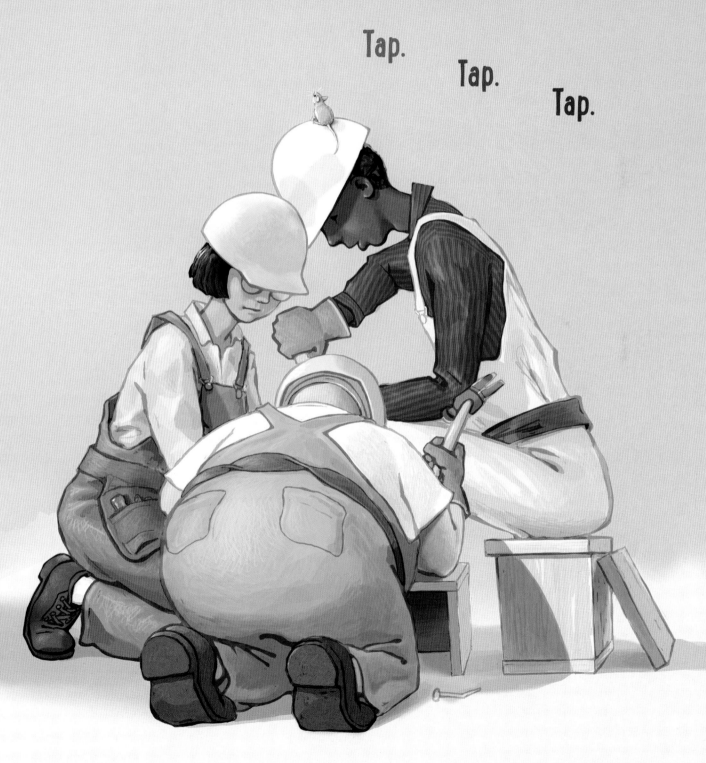

Up they go, and now we're done.
Little homes for everyone!
In groups of two, in groups of three,
they swoop and skitter down to see.

Every critter claims a box . . .

And there she stands.
The queen of clocks.

To my builder brother Ken

hmhbooks.com

The text type was set in Amasis MT Std.
The display type was set in LunchBox.

Design by Andrea Miller

Library of Congress Cataloging-in-Publication Data

Names: Cyrus, Kurt, author, illustrator.
Title: Fix that clock! / Kurt Cyrus.
Description: Boston ; New York : Houghton Mifflin Harcourt, [2019] | Summary:
A construction crew rebuilds an old clock tower that has become home to
rats, bats, mice, and an assortment of birds.
Identifiers: LCCN 2018052145 | ISBN 9781328904089 (hardcover picture book)
Subjects: | CYAC: Stories in rhyme. | Buildings—Repair and
reconstruction—Fiction. | Rodents—Fiction. | Birds—Fiction.
Classification: LCC PZ8.3.C997 Fix 2019 | DDC [E]—dc23
LC record available at https://lccn.loc.gov/2018052145

ISBN: 978-1-328-90408-9

Manufactured in China
SCP 10 9 8 7 6 5 4 3 2 1
4500772268